Oliver
and the
Wishing
Star

Jennifer
Decker

Chrish
Vindhy

To my family and friends,
and to everyone who ever wished
they were someone else.

The grass beneath your feet is
greener than you think.

A very special thank you to

my Editor, Brooke Vitale and my Book Designer, Tia Perkin.

978-1-7377644-0-3

Library of Congress Control Number: 2021917137

"BYE, MOM!"

Oliver shouted.
"I'm going swimming at Finn's house!
I'll be back for dinner!"

Oliver reached for the doorknob.
He was almost there. Almost free!
And then he heard it—

"Not so fast.

Do you have any homework?"

Oliver groaned.
"Yes," he admitted.
"But I'll finish it when I get back! I promise!"

Oliver's mom folded her arms and began tapping her foot. He knew that look. It was not good.

"Oliver, do you remember the last time I let you go over to Finn's house without finishing your homework? How you were up way past your bedtime—way past *my* bedtime! In fact, I seem to recall you fell asleep in class that very next day!"

"But, MOM!"
pleaded Oliver.

"But Mom, nothing," she said. "Why don't you take Cooper for a walk and then you can start your homework before dinner."

Sighing, Oliver looped the leash over Cooper's head. It was so unfair. How come he had to miss out on having fun just because his lousy teacher gave him homework? What was so important about homework, anyway?

"Dogs never have homework," he said as he walked. "In fact, dogs don't have any responsibilities!

You've got it so easy, Cooper, and I'm... Cursed!"

The farther they went, the more Oliver thought about the idea of being a dog.

"I know we're supposed to be the dogs' masters, but who's really barking orders? You want to go for a walk? We take you for a walk! You want food? We give you food! And when you're done doing your business outside, who gets stuck cleaning it up?

WE DO! I DO!"

Suddenly, Oliver realized he'd reached the corner. He eyed the crosswalk. He wasn't supposed to cross the street alone, but who was going to stop him?

"No one, that's who!"

Oliver looked left, then right, then left again. And then…he defiantly stepped off the curb.

But breaking the rules wasn't any more fun than following them, and he quickly turned around.

"Cooper, you don't know how lucky you are," Oliver said a bit later.

"No homework, no chores, no having to eat broccoli, YUCK!

You don't even have to say excuse me when you let one *rip*!"

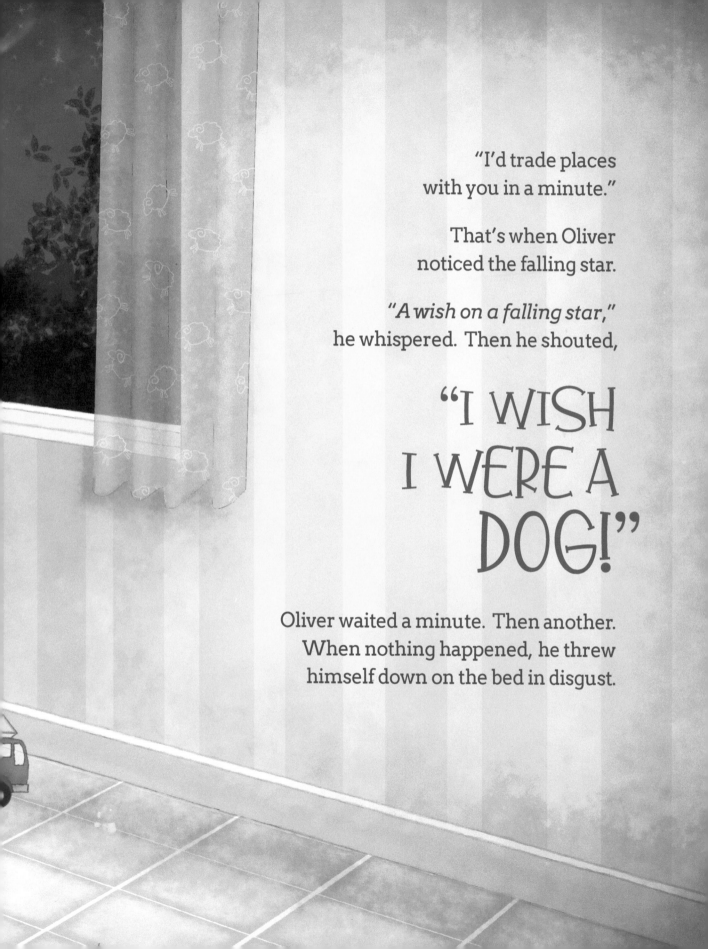

"I'd trade places
with you in a minute."

That's when Oliver
noticed the falling star.

"A wish on a falling star,"
he whispered. Then he shouted,

"I WISH
I WERE A
DOG!"

Oliver waited a minute. Then another.
When nothing happened, he threw
himself down on the bed in disgust.

A little while later, Oliver awoke to the sound of
Cooper **growling**.

"What's the matter, boy?"

he asked.

Then Oliver spied himself in the mirror.
He couldn't believe it. He'd really turned into
a dog! His wish had come true!

Oliver looked around. He had to get out of there before Mom spotted him. He quickly hopped out the window and set off down the street.

"This is too cool!" shouted Oliver.

"I'm a free man! I mean, dog!"

But Oliver's happiness didn't last long.
The darker it got, the colder it got, and soon
it began to rain. The wind howled and
Oliver's stomach began to

growl.

That's when he heard Old Lady Brewster. She was well known for having a soft spot for strays.

"Hi there, Pup.
I've got some food for you."

Oliver bounded forward,
excited for a snack.

But as he leaned in, a
terrible smell hit his nose.

"GROSS!

I'm not eating *dog* food!"
Oliver barked.

"What is it, boy? Aren't you
hungry," asked the old woman.

Oliver jumped off the front porch and headed home. Maybe, somehow, his mom would recognize him. But when he got home, he found his parents eating without him.

"They didn't even notice I'm gone," he sniffed.

Head hung low, Oliver backed away from the window. He was so busy feeling sorry for himself that he didn't pay attention to where he was. Then, suddenly—

"GOTCHA!"

Oliver screamed for the dogcatcher to let him go, but no words came. Instead, the only sound was barking. Oliver saw his life flash before his eyes. How he wished this was all a bad dream.

"MOMMY!"

Oliver screamed.
"MOMMY! HELP ME!"

"OLIVER! WAKE UP!"

screamed his mom.

Oliver opened his eyes. He was back home in his room.

"That must have been some crazy dream," Oliver's mom said. "You were tearing at your sheets, calling out to me."

"It wasn't a dream! I was a dog! There was this star! I made a wish. It was *real!*"

"Oh, Oliver. You just had a bad dream. Come on. Dinner's ready."

Oliver rubbed his eyes.

With one last kiss on the head, Mom left Oliver's room. Throwing off his covers, he hopped out of bed and gasped. His feet and sheets were completely covered with *mud*!

"It wasn't a dream."

That night at dinner Oliver's dad asked if he would say grace. Oliver nodded.

"Dear God, thank you for this food we are about to receive. Thank you, for my mom and dad, and thank you for not making me a dog! AMEN!"

Oliver's mom and dad looked at each other, and then at Oliver.

"What was that last thing you said, Oliver?" asked his dad.

"Oh, nothing,"

Oliver said.

And as he stuffed his mouth full of spaghetti, he made himself a promise to never again wish he were anyone—or anything—else.

He was Oliver, and that was pretty good!